Sea Billows

Story by

Jill Watson Glassco

Copyright Page

Sea Billows, Copyright © 2018 Jill Watson Glassco

Illustrations: Anya Figert

Cover art: Megan Roberts

Cover design: Ben Glassco

Printed and Published in the United States of America

ISBN-13: 978-1939535290

ISBN: 1939535298

www.DeepSeaPublishing.com

Table of Contents

For babygrand #7

We can't wait for you to hatch.

"For the LORD God is our sun and our shield.

He gives us grace and glory.

The LORD will withhold no good thing

From those who do what is right."

(Psalm 84:11)

Chapter 1
Homeward Bound

Marina pushed her oversized head above the salty foam and gulped air through strong jaws and two round nostrils in a hard, thick beak.

WHOOSH!

One powerful down stroke of long, paddle-shaped fore-flippers propelled the loggerhead sea turtle three body lengths forward.

WHOOSH!

WHOOSHHH!

She glided gracefully under the ocean swells like a soaring eagle over puffy clouds. Using hind-flippers as rudders, Marina steered toward the ocean floor and ignored the playful dolphin circling around and around and around the determined turtle.

FUEL.

The two-hundred-eighty-seven-pound reptile needed fuel for her urgent mission and long journey. She navigated delicate coral branches and pink-tinged sea fans and cruised over a seafloor smorgasbord of clams, mussels, and sea urchins toward a spiny lobster.

SNAP!

CRUNCH!

The cat-and-mouse chase ends. Marina is fed and fueled. For thirty-three years, this saltwater beauty aimlessly explored hundreds of miles of the Gulf of Mexico and open seas of the North Atlantic. But, today, one particular beach tugs at Marina's heart like a strong magnet on an iron key, drawing her back to a distant memory. In the wake of years and years of migration, Marina charts her course toward home.

Scientists scratch their heads. Marine biologists marvel. How does a mother sea turtle find her way back to the same beach where she hatched to lay her eggs? Some claim the females rely on the Earth's magnetic field to draw them home. Others think that hatchlings imprint the qualities of their natal beach and relocate it by its unique characteristics such as smell and sound. A few propose that younger sea turtles follow the older reptiles home. Yet another slice of humanity believes that the simple secret is revealed in the oldest book of the Bible. *For the LORD answered Job from a whirlwind:*

"Who is this that questions My wisdom with such ignorant words," God said. *"Where were you when I laid the foundations of the earth? Tell Me, if you know so much. Who determined its dimensions and stretched out the surveying line? What supports its foundation, and who laid its cornerstone as the morning stars sang together and all the angels shouted for joy?"*

"Who kept the sea inside its boundaries as it burst from the womb, and as I clothed it with clouds and wrapped it in thick darkness? For I locked it behind barred gates, limiting its shores. I said, 'This

far and no farther will you come. Here you proud waves must stop.'"

"Have you ever commanded the morning to appear and caused the dawn to rise in the east? Can you direct the movement of the stars – binding the cluster of the Pleiades or loosening the cords of Orion? Can you direct the constellations through the seasons or guide the bear with her cubs across the heavens?"

"Who provides food for the ravens when their young cry out to God and wander about in hunger? Have you given the horse its strength or clothed its neck with a flowing mane? Is it your strength that makes the hawk soar and spread its wings toward the south?"

These believers in the word of God trust that Almighty God, who laid the foundations of the world, kept the sea in its boundaries, commanded the morning to appear, directed the movement of the constellations, provided food for the ravens, gave the horse its mane, and made the hawk soar, also made sea turtles and gave the females the innate ability to return to their birth home.

WHOOSH!

WHOOSHH!

WHOOSHHH!

Marina oared toward the sunlight zone. At rest, she can easily stay underwater four to seven hours, but foraging and swimming, she must breathe every five to ten minutes. On the surface, the turtle stretched out her flippers, exposing her reddish-brown upper shell or carapace to the warm sunshine, and gently rocked back and forth, back and forth on a calm ocean. Overhead, a squadron of cackling pelicans in perfect V formation sailed across a spring sky as blue as the robin's egg, announcing that Fort Morgan is less than a hundred miles ahead.

Alabama's historic Fort Morgan straddles a narrow peninsula in Baldwin County where the Gulf of Mexico and Mobile Bay collide and served as a military post across the Civil War through World War II. The U.S. Corps of Engineers built the star-shaped, masonry fortification in the early 1800s to replace Fort Bowyer, an earthen stockade attacked by the British forces twice in the War of 1812. Today, beach houses and high-rise condominiums line the sugar-sand beaches where Marina hatched over thirty years ago.

Refueled, rested, and refreshed, Marina pressed on.

REFLECTIONS

Life is a journey, dear reader, and God Almighty who commanded the dawn to appear and gave mother sea turtles the innate ability to return to their birth home made you.

_____ (your name), I made all the delicate, inner parts of your body and knit you together in your mother's womb. My workmanship is marvelous. I saw you before you were born. Every day of your life is recorded in My book. Every moment was laid out before a single day had passed. (Psalm 139:13-16)

_____(your name), you are My masterpiece. In Christ Jesus, I create you anew, so you can do good things I planned for you long ago. (Ephesians 2:10)

_____ (your name), I know the plans I have for you – good plans to give you a future and a hope. When you pray, I listen. When you look for Me wholeheartedly, you will find Me. (Jeremiah 29:11-13)

You, _____(your name), matter to God.

Chapter 2:
Eggs and Izzy

Days later, a cherry-red sun dropped under the western horizon. Egg-laden Marina swam the final lane of her land-bound journey and reached the water's edge in darkness. Her graceful sea waltz slowed to an awkward crawl up the shore and past the high-tide line. The loggerhead probed the sand with her snout and then lifted her head and surveyed the beachscape. With alternating flipper motions, she dragged her pale-yellow underbelly or plastron toward her destiny. The sea turtle paused to rest and then resumed the laborious trek.

She bulldozed NORTH.

REST.

Plowed WEST.

REST.

Pushed NORTH.

CLANG!

At the sea oat line, Marina's iron will hit home, and the mother turtle began preparing the body pit to lay her eggs. First, she cleared the site with solid sweeps of her fore-flippers. Next, alternately using her smaller, back flippers, she scooped one cupful of sand after another, laying it beside the nesting site. Unbeknownst to the busy, determined mother, a tiny lizard watched in the distance.

When she could dig no deeper, the sea turtle painstakingly scraped the sides of the cavity to any remove loose sand. The egg chamber – measuring nineteen inches deep, nine inches in diameter at the bottom, and seven inches in diameter at the top – was completed, at last.

In a focused trance, one by one, Marina dropped 109 perfectly round, pliable-shelled, ivory-white eggs into the chamber and then covered the freshly laid clutch with sand. The large reptile carefully packed down each scoop with her flippers and tightly compressed the sandy soil by rocking her heavy body from side to side over the top. To camouflage the nest from sea-turtle-egg predators such as raccoons, dogs, and people, she tossed additional heaps of sand over a broad area. Exhausted, the turtle sluggishly turned around and…

RESTED.

When strength returned, Marina retraced her telltale tracks to the water, crawled into the surf, and glided out to sea. Purely by happenstance would this mother ever lay eyes on her hatchlings.

~

Seven weeks later.

Jacob Fickle trapped the tiny lizard between his palm and the boardwalk. "Hey, Mom, I found a baby lizard," he called.

Rebekah snapped another shot of the white-breasted seagull tip-toeing through shallow waves and answered, "Bring it here, buddy, and let me see."

Ten-year-old Elizabeth brushed the sand from her hands and knees and ran toward her eleven-year-old brother. "I wanna see!" she cried.

Jacob opened his fist. Rebekah pointed the Canon camera lens toward the quarter-size lizard clinging to his fingers.

SNAP!

SNAP!

SNAP!

Elizabeth sighed. "Oh, it's sooo cute."

Martha Willowkins peered over her grandson's shoulder. "I've never seen such a teensy lizard," she said. "What should we name it?"

Wilbur affectionately kissed his wife's cheek. "Martha, you think *every* critter on God's green earth has to have a name," he teased.

Like clockwork, every other June, Wilbur and Martha Willowkins rent the same three-story beach house at Fort Morgan, Alabama for a fun vacation with their children and grandchildren. This summer, Granny, their son-in-law's grandmother, had joined the family holiday.

Elizabeth studied the small, brown creature with a curly tail and a head too big for its slender body sitting perfectly still in her brother's hand.

"Izzy," she announced.

"Izzy," repeated Martha. "I like that. Itsy-bitsy Izzy."

"Can we keep it?" Elizabeth begged. "Pleeease, Mom?"

"No, baby. God put everything lizards need to grow and thrive right here on the beach. We better let her go. Take Izzy back to where you found her, Jacob."

"Okay," said Jacob.

"Bye, Itsy-bitsy Izzy," moaned Elizabeth.

Jacob opened his fingers. The brown anole raced across the sand and disappeared under the boardwalk. Although Izzy's species – Anolis sagrei – are native to Cuba and the Bahamas, the lizards invaded the southern United States via pet stores and are now commonly seen darting in and out and over and around tall sea oats and gnarled scrub pines on Alabama beaches.

"Who wants to play bocce ball?" asked Isaac, Jacob and Elizabeth's eight-year-old brother.

"I do," said Jacob.

"Me, too," said Stephen, their dad.

"I'll play," said Dan Willowkins.

"I'm on Uncle Dan's team!" cried Isaac.

"Come on, Jacob," said Stephen. "Uncle Dan and Isaac are goin' down."

"I'm first," said Isaac.

"No, I'm first," Jacob insisted.

Wilbur pulled a nickel from his pocket. "Heads or tails, Jacob," he said.

"Heads," called Jacob.

Wilbur tossed the coin into the air; it plopped heads-down on the sand.

"Tails! I'm first," shouted Isaac.

Jacob shrugged. "Oh, well. I'm green," he said.

"Okay. I'm red," said Isaac.

"I'll be blue," said Dan.

"Guess I'm yellow," said Stephen.

Dan threw the target ball up the beach. "First team to sixteen wins," he said.

Jacob's green ball sailed past the target into the sea oats and dropped beside a wooden stake with a small, yellow sign stapled to the top. He picked up the ball and read aloud:

DO NOT DISTURB

SEA TURTLE NEST

VIOLATORS SUBJECT

TO FINES AND

IMPRISONMENT

US ENDANGERED SPECIES ACT OF 1973

MARKED: May 5, 2017

REFLECTIONS

Your life, _____ (your name), has

purpose. Almighty God, who forged the strong pull of a magnet on

an iron key and planted the powerful draw of a birth beach in

Marina's heart, also placed His purpose in you.

~

_____ (your name), I knew you before I

formed you in your mother's womb. Before you were born, I set

you apart [for My purpose]. (Jeremiah 1:5)

_____ (your name), I have appointed

you for the very purpose of displaying My power in you and to

spread My fame throughout the earth. (Romans 9:17)

So, run with purpose, _____ (your name),

in every step. (1 Corinthians 9:26a)

~

God created you, _____ (your name),

on purpose and for His purpose.

Chapter 3:
Day Forty-nine

"Hey, Uncle Ben," shouted Jacob, "here's a sea turtle nest!"

Ben Willowkins, picked up one-year-old Hunter and grabbed three-year-old Alexander's hand. "C'mon, boys," he said. "Let's go see a turtle nest."

"It's dated May fifth," said Wilbur.

"Cinco de Mayo," said Ben.

"How long does it take turtle eggs to hatch?" asked Rebekah.

Stephen searched his smart phone and reported, "Six to nine weeks, and May fifth was one, two, three…right at seven weeks ago."

"So, the eggs could hatch this week!" cried Amanda Willowkins, Dan's wife. She kissed one-year-old baby Lee. "You might get to see some baby sea turtles, buddy."

"That'd be cool," said Ben's wife, Gabriela.

Elizabeth turned a cartwheel. "Oh, I hope so! I *love* sea turtles."

"Who put up the sign?" asked Isaac. "And how'd they know this is a turtle nest? I don't see anything but sand."

"Well, since sea turtles are endangered, people volunteer to help protect them," said Stephen. "The group around here is called Share the Beach. They patrol the beaches day and night and mark the turtle nests."

"How'd you know that?" asked Rebekah.

Stephen grinned and pointed to his phone. "And here's the number to call to report a sea turtle emergency."

"Okay," said Martha. "Everybody run clean up for dinner. We leave in one hour. It's seafood tonight!"

"Papaw, can we go crab huntin' after supper?" asked Jacob.

"Of course," said Wilbur.

The tall and small marched over the boardwalk to the beach house, leaving Marina's clutch hidden beneath the sign. Across the weeks, the eggs had passed through twenty-nine of thirty-one stages of embryonic development. The first six stages took place even before the mother sea turtle dropped her wonders into the egg chamber.

Twelve days after her return to the ocean – stage twenty-one – the tiny embryos' heads and eyes had formed, and by day eighteen, upper shells were recognizable. In recent days, their amazing transformation had accelerated, and now, the very active pre-hatchlings sported a caruncle or egg tooth, which at the appointed time is used to break out of their shells. In merely forty-nine days, Marina's eggs had miraculously metamorphosed from tiny cells to four-flippered, shell-covered, soon-to-hatch sea turtles.

The world labels extraordinary events *outside* natural or scientific laws as miracles; but truth be told, remarkable miracles within nature's laws (written by extraordinary God) occur every day among every tribe, tongue, people, and nation around the globe. In a psalm of David, the King of Israel sang:

"O LORD, You have examined my heart

and know everything about me.

Such knowledge is too wonderful for me,

too great for me to understand!

You made all the delicate, inner parts of my body

and knit me together in my mother's womb.

You saw me before I was born.

Every day of my life was recorded in Your book.

Every moment laid out before a single day had passed.

How precious are Your thoughts about me, O God.

They cannot be numbered!"

(Psalm 139)

Day forty-nine faded. The fiery sun dropped from the sky and a first-quarter moon rose over the Gulf of Mexico. Its dim glow cast delicate, silver crowns atop pounding waves. Proud sea oats bowed to the strong, south wind, and hungry Izzy zigzagged the shifting dunes on hunt for ants or spiders or mealworms. From the shadows, a masked bandit – one of the greatest threats to Marina's eggs – stole quietly toward the nest.

Jacob trapped the intruder in the beam of his flashlight and yelled, "Hey, get away from there, Mr. Raccoon."

The old predator trotted into the darkness, determined to return at a more opportune time. For the most part, raccoons wreak havoc on a sea turtle nest at two stages: either the first days of the fresh laid clutch or the post-emergent stage after the hatchlings crawl to the surface and rush to the water. So, for tonight, the eggs remained safe and sound in their sand-and-shell refuge.

"Shine your light over here, Elizabeth," said Martha, pointing along the water's edge.

"Wow!" cried Elizabeth.

Dozens of sand crabs scurried over the beach. The nocturnal (more active in the dark of the night than light of the day) crustaceans appeared pale and ghostly, befitting their nickname:

ghost crab. One darted between Elizabeth's feet. The little girl squealed.

"There it goes!" yelled Wilbur. "Grab it with the net, Jacob."

"I found a big one," called Dan. "Where's the bucket?"

"I've got it," said Martha.

Gabriela tried to set Hunter on the beach, but the baby lifted both legs high into the air. She laughed and said, "He doesn't like the sand on his feet."

"He'll get used to it," said Amanda. "It took Lee awhile. Now look at him."

Baby Lee played happily in the sand with a toy shovel in each chubby hand. Alexander sprawled on his belly beside him eying a small crab burrowing into the seashore.

Ben's Moto Force Droid beeped. "Did y'all know we're under a tropical storm warning? We better enjoy the beach tomorrow. Tropical Storm Cindy's predicted to come ashore the day after."

REFLECTIONS

Undoubtedly, storms *will* crash into your life, _____ (your name), but you are never alone. Unlike a mother sea turtle and her hatchlings, Jesus never abandons a heart that belongs to Him.

~

_____ (your name), I have told you all this so that you may have peace in Me. Here on earth you will have many trials and sorrows. But take heart, because I have overcome the world. (John 16:33)

Don't be afraid, _____ (your name), for I am with you. Don't be discouraged, for I am your God. I will strengthen you and help you. I will hold you up with My victorious right hand. (Isaiah 41:10)

So, you can say with confidence, _____ (your name), the Lord is my helper, so I will have no fear. What can mere people do to me? (Hebrews 13:6)

~

In Jesus Christ, _____ (your name), you are never alone.

Chapter 4:
Day Fifty

"Turn it up, please, so I can hear what they're saying," said Wilbur the next morning.

"Tropical Storm Cindy is churning slowly toward the US Gulf Coast," reported the meteorologist, "where millions of residents are expecting heavy rain and potential flash flooding. At least seventeen million people are under a tropical storm warning form San Luis Pass, Texas, to the Alabama-Florida border. The storm could bring up to fifteen inches of rain in parts of southeastern Louisiana, southern Mississippi, southern Alabama, and western portions of the Florida Panhandle through Thursday night. A few tornadoes and inundation of one to three feet along the coast are also possible.

"What does inundation mean?" asked Jacob.

"It means there could be flooding. The sea level could rise one to three feet," said Stephen.

"What'll happen to the turtle eggs?" asked Elizabeth.

Rebekah and Martha exchanged concerned glances.

"Well, sugar," said Martha, "if the tide rises over the nest, it could damage it or possibly wash the eggs out to sea."

"Oh, no!" wailed Elizabeth.

Martha patted Elizabeth's hand. "Now, don't you fret, honey. God tells us to pray instead of worry and to trust Him no matter what happens."

"Yes, ma'am," she said. "But…"

"No buts, young lady. Trust God," Martha repeated.

"Can we still go to Blake's birthday party?" Isaac asked.

"Sure," said Dan. "It's windy, but it's not supposed to start raining till tonight."

"Good," said Isaac. "I love baseball."

By design, the grandchildren's seven-year-old cousin, Blake, was vacationing with his grandparents thirty miles down the coast at Orange Beach and had invited the Willowkins, Fickles, and Granny to his beach-baseball birthday party.

At the party, Martha yelled over the crashing waves, "We wanna pitcher not a cement mixer!"

Her brother, Franklin Woollyworth, flung a strike over home plate.

"Strike two," Ben called.

"Keep your eye on the ball, Mimi," Blake encouraged.

Third pitch, Lynn Woollyworth hit the ball to left field and sped toward first. Three feet from the driftwood base, she tumbled into the sand, but somehow managed to slap first before Dan tagged her.

"Safe!" called Wilbur.

Gabriela and Amanda sat nearby under a broad umbrella watching the three toddlers fill plastic buckets. When Alexander emptied his orange pail, a ghost crab scrambled out of the sand pile.

"Mamaw, a cwab was hidin' in my bucket!" Alexander shouted to Martha, who was waiting in line to bat. "Silly cwab."

"He's a sneaky one," called Martha. "Sneaky Pete, the ghost crab."

Alexander cocked his head to one side and studied Sneaky Pete's black eyes on elongated stalks and two front claws, one visibly larger than the other. When the little boy touched its box-like back, the crab burrowed out of sight in a wink.

"Silly Sneaky Pete,"

he said.

DRIP.

DROP.

DRIP.

Raindrops polka-dotted dry sand.

"The storm must be coming in faster than they thought," said Lynn. "I guess it's time for birthday cake."

Inside the condo, the household sang:

"Happy birthday to you,

Happy birthday to you,

Happy birthday, dear Blake,

Happy birthday to you!"

Martha announced, "Kids, I hate to be a party pooper, but try to finish up the delicious cake and ice cream as fast as you can.

We need to head on back to the beach house to batten down the hatches before Cindy's landfall. I'm sorry we have to rush off like this, Lynn."

"I understand," said Lynn. "Y'all be careful."

Martha hugged her sister-in-law. "Y'all, too. Thanks for inviting us. We love you all so much!"

At Fort Morgan, Stephen and Rebekah folded chairs and stacked them in the wagon on top of the floats and beach toys. Ben grabbed the kayak.

"I told you we should have put everything up before we left," said Wilbur.

"Yeah, but we didn't know the storm would come in this fast," said Dan.

"You think the tents will hold up in this wind?" asked Martha.

"It's the rental company's call whether to leave 'em up or take 'em down," said Wilbur. "They're used to these storms. They'll know what to do."

Deep purple and yellow clouds boiled over the gulf. A strong gust sent an umbrella cartwheeling down the beach like tumbleweed over the desert. Red flags snapped in the stiff breeze warning swimmers of hazardous riptides under the swollen surf.

Cindy, the third tropical storm of the season, swirled about 265 miles south of Morgan City, Louisiana with sustained winds of forty-five miles per hour. With threats of torrential rains and possible tornadoes, Alabama Governor Kay Ivey issued a state of emergency and warned vacationers to stay out of the deadly waves.

Sheets of rain slapped the beach house windows, and Izzy hunkered under the boardwalk. A flock of seagulls flew low over the turbulent surf, and a pelican V rode the forceful winds inland. Marina's clutch, however, sat calmly in the sand – oblivious to the approaching threat to survival.

REFLECTIONS

_____ (your name), like the sand-and-shell refuge, Jesus is your peace in life storms.

~

_____ (your name), I will be a shelter from daytime heat and a hiding place from the storms and rain. (Isaiah 4:6)

Don't let your heart be troubled, _____ (your name). Trust Me. (John 14:1)

I am leaving you, _____ (your name), with a gift – peace of mind and heart. And the peace I give you is a gift the world cannot give. So, don't be troubled or afraid. (John 14:27)

~

_____ (your name), you can find peace in Jesus, even in turbulent times.

Chapter 5:

Empires

"Alexander and Hunter are finally asleep," said Gabriela.

"Lee went out like a light," said Amanda. "He was *so* tired."

"Let's have a game night!" said Isaac.

"Y'all wanna play Empires?" asked Dan.

"I've never heard of Empires," said Granny. "How do you play?"

"So, there's a question and everybody writes down the answer," said Elizabeth.

"And you have to guess everybody's answer," said Isaac.

"And whoever builds the biggest empire wins," said Jacob.

"Okay," said Stephen, "let me explain the rules to Granny. So, the whole group decides on a question and everyone writes down their secret answer to the question. Then a designated reader collects all the answers and reads them aloud twice to the group. The person to the left of the reader goes first and tries to match a person with their corresponding answer. If he guesses correctly, the guesser becomes a king and the person he guessed is captured and joins his "empire," and then he asked another person. The guesser or king continues guessing as long as he is correct. When his guess is wrong, the person he guessed incorrectly takes control, and it's his or her turn to guess. Guessing a king's answer correctly captures that king and as well as his entire empire. The game ends when one of the kings figures out all the answers and captures all of his opponents, completing the empire. Does that make sense?"

Granny smiled. "Kinda."

"You'll catch on as we play," Martha said. "It's not hard."

Rebekah handed out pencils and small slips of paper. "What's the first question?" she asked.

"How about what animal would you like to be on a carousel?" said Jacob.

"Or what's your favorite Bible character?" said Martha. "Other than Jesus, of course."

"I know," said Elizabeth. "What would you name a baby sea turtle?"

"Yeah," said Amanda. "Let's do that one. How many eggs are in a sea turtle nest anyhow?"

Dan looked at his wife. "That's random," he teased.

"Anywhere from fifty to 200. The average is 110," said Ben.

"How do you know?" asked Dan.

"Oh, believe me. Ben knows. He watches nature shows all the time," said Gabriela.

"Does everyone agree, then?" asked Rebekah. "What would you name a baby sea turtle?"

"Sure."

"Yeah."

"Sounds good to me."

"I'll be the designated reader. So, Dan, you're the first guesser," said Rebekah.

"Alright!" said Dan.

Rebekah read, "Okay, the answers to 'what would you name a baby sea turtle' are: Rudder, Star, Boom, Hadi, Lily, Bella, Joe, Nemo, Keel, Cindy, Punch, and Jack Sparrow. One more time: Rudder, Star, Boom, Hadi, Lily, Bella, Joe, Nemo, Keel, Cindy, Punch, and Jack Sparrow. Dan, you go first."

"Amanda," said Dan. "did you say Lily?"

"Yes," said Amanda. "How'd you guess?"

"Because that's what you wanted to name Bell when she showed up at the Coosa River farm. Come on, wife. You're in my empire, and I'm your king," he joked.

Amanda laughed. She and Dan conferred in whispers.

"Mama, did you say Cindy?" guessed Dan.

Martha grinned. "Nope!"

"Awww man!" said Dan.

Martha took control.

"Wilbur, did you say Joe?" she said.

Wilbur laughed. "Yep."

"I should've known that one," said Dan.

"Who's Joe?" asked Granny.

"Joe was the name of our black lab we had for fifteen years," said Martha. "He was such a smart dog. So, Granny, did you say Cindy?"

"Yes, I did," said Granny. "After the storm and my daughter, Cindy."

"Who do you think said Nemo?" Martha whispered to Wilbur and Granny.

"One of the kids," whispered Wilbur. "Ask Elizabeth."

"Elizabeth," said Martha. "Did you say Nemo?"

"No," said Elizabeth. "My turn."

"Isaac, did you say Nemo?" said Elizabeth.

"Yeah," said Isaac, and then he whispered to Elizabeth, "I think Dad or Uncle Ben said Jack Sparrow."

"Let's try Dad," she whispered. "Dad, did you say Jack Sparrow?"

Stephen grinned. "Nope. My turn. Jacob, did you say Jack Sparrow?"

"Yes," said Jacob.

"And, Dan, did you say Boom?" said Stephen.

"Argh! Yes," said Dan. "Come on, Amanda. He got both of us."

"Rebekah, did you say Hadi?" said Stephen.

"Of course," she answered.

"How'd you know, Dad?" asked Isaac.

"Because if Jacob had been a girl, your mom wanted to name her Hadassah and call her Hadi," said Stephen.

"Glad I'm a boy," said Jacob.

Rebekah made a face at her oldest boy.

"Come on, y'all. We gotta stop Stephen," said Ben. "He's about to win."

"Okay, Ben, did you say Rudder?" said Stephen.

"Yes. How'd you figure that out? I didn't think anybody would guess that I said Rudder," Ben moaned.

"Process of elimination," said Stephen. "I didn't think you said Bella or Star."

"How'd you come up with Rudder?" asked Gabriela.

"It's a nautical term – part of a sailboat," said Ben.

"Ben," whispered Stephen, "what would Gabriela say?"

"She probably said Bella," whispered Ben. "That's her niece's name."

"Gabriela, did you say Bella?" said Stephen.

"Yeah," said Gabriela.

"Okay, who's left and what answers?" Stephen whispered to his captives.

"Keel, Punch…"

"I'm Punch," whispered Stephen.

"Okay, then, we're down to Elizabeth and Mamaw for Star and Keel," said Ben.

"Elizabeth has to be Star, and Mamaw must be Keel," whispered Stephen. "Elizabeth, did you say Star?"

"Yes, sir."

"And, Mamaw, you said Keel," Stephen declared triumphantly.

"Yes," said Martha. "Game over. King Stephen is the winner!"

Later that night, Elizabeth snuggled under the covers and silently prayed, *Thank You, Lord, for my family, and thank You for letting us come to the beach. Please keep us safe in the storm, and please protect the turtle eggs and Izzy, too. Amen.*

REFLECTIONS

_____ (your name), the Bible clearly teaches that two empires or kingdoms are warring for your allegiance: The Kingdom of God and Satan's kingdom of darkness.

~

_____ (your name), seek first the Kingdom of God above all else, and live righteously, and I will give you everything you need. (Matthew 6:33)

_____ (your name), the Kingdom of God is near! Repent of your sins and believe My Good News. [Jesus died for your sins and rose again]. (Mark 1:15)

For I will rescue you from the kingdom of darkness, _____ (your name), and transfer you into the Kingdom of My dear Son. (Colossians 1:13)

~

_____ (your name), rest assured, Jesus, the Prince of Peace, is greater, stronger, and higher than Satan, the prince of darkness. God wins! Jesus will reign as King of kings and Lord of lords forever and ever and ever.

Chapter 6:
Day Fifty-one

The following gray morning, Martha salted and peppered a dozen scrambled eggs while Wilbur fried two pounds of bacon and a pound of hot sausage in iron skillets.

The morning news blared. "Cindy made landfall in Cameron Parish, Louisiana between 2:00 and 4:00 a.m. Central Daylight Time with maximum sustained winds between forty and forty-five miles per hour," reported the meteorologist. "Even though downgraded to a tropical depression, heavy rainfall and severe thunderstorms continue to extend well out from the center of the storm, especially along the gulf coast of Mississippi and Alabama. Some areas have already received eight to ten inches of rain, and residents along the coast are advised to watch for possible tornadoes and waterspouts throughout today and tonight. The radar indicates a sixty percent chance of possible clearing by noon tomorrow as the storm pushes inland."

"Have you looked at the beach?" asked Martha. "The tents are completely demolished. There's nothing but poles standing. I feel bad for the rental company."

"Yeah," said Wilbur, "me too. And the tide's over the turtle nest."

"Oh, no," moaned Martha.

"Nothing we can do until the storm moves out and the tide drops," he said. "Here come the troops."

Jacob and Isaac tramped down the stairs.

"Mmm," said Isaac. "Smells good."

"Can I have two sausage and cheese biscuits, Mamaw?" asked Jacob.

"Sure, honey," said Martha. "Everything should be ready in about five minutes. Did you sleep well last night or did the storm wake you up?"

"I slept good," he said. "Alexander, Hunter, and Lee are still sleeping."

"Is Elizabeth asleep, too?" asked Martha.

"No, ma'am. She's not in her bed. I don't know where she is," said Jacob.

"Maybe she's in Rebekah and Stephen's room," said Wilbur.

Rebekah walked into the kitchen. "Good morning. Anything I can do to help?" she asked.

"Rebekah, have you seen Elizabeth?" asked Martha. "The boys said she's up, but she hasn't come downstairs."

"Maybe she's in the bathroom. I'll go check." Rebekah said and walked back upstairs.

"She's not up here," Rebekah called down. "Jacob, go check downstairs, please."

"She's not down here either, Mom," Jacob hollered from the first floor.

"Stephen, we can't find Elizabeth," Rebekah cried.

"What do you mean you can't find her?" said Stephen.

Rebekah's voice quavered. "She's not in her bed. She's not in any of the bathrooms, and we've searched all three floors and can't find her anywhere. Where could she be?"

"Don't panic. Run see if her tennis shoes and jacket are in her room," said Stephen, quickly tying his sneakers and pulling a hooded slicker over his head. "And check the house one more time."

"Surely she didn't go outside in this storm!" said Rebekah.

"Elizabeth!" called Martha.

Wilbur dashed upstairs and grabbed his shoes and jacket.

"What's going on?" asked Ben.

"We can't find Elizabeth," said Wilbur.

Dan ran up the steps to the kitchen. "What's wrong?" he asked.

"Elizabeth is missing," cried Martha.

"Missing?" said Dan.

"We can't find her anywhere in the house," said Martha.

"Do you think she went to the beach to check the turtle nest?" asked Dan.

"I hope not! Have you seen the beach?" gasped Martha. "Should I call 911?"

Stephen, Ben, and Wilbur hurried into the kitchen.

"We'll check the beach first. If she's not there, Mama, call 911," Dan ordered.

The men opened the sliding glass door. A blast of wind sailed paper plates and napkins from the table. Baby Lee began to cry.

"Y'all be careful!" said Amanda, fighting back her own tears.

"Lord Jesus, please help us find Elizabeth," Martha prayed.

Rain and sand blew sideways stinging the men's faces and bare legs like tiny needles. Stephen led the charge down the gravel driveway and onto the slippery boardwalk.

TROMP.

TROMP.

TROMP trotted soaked tennis shoes over the wet planks. The rising tide lapped the end of the walkway.

"ELIZABETH!!!"

Stephen's shout evaporated into the thrashing waves and gale-force winds.

Dan jumped over the railing and dropped to his hands and knees. Below the walkway crouched a whimpering little girl under a soggy, lavender parka.

"Found her!" he yelled.

"Uncle D...Dan! I...I just wanted...I wanted to check on the eggs," Elizabeth sobbed. "And I couldn't get...get to the nest becau...because the waves were too high. And I couldn't...I couldn't get back to house, and I was s...so scared."

"It's okay, Elizabeth. I've got you." Dan gathered his trembling niece into his arms. "I've got you."

REFLECTIONS

_____ (your name), everyone needs a Rescuer.

~

For everyone has sinned; we all fall short of God's glorious standard. (Romans 3:23) The wages of sin is death, _____ (your name), but the free gift of God is eternal life through Jesus Christ our Lord. (Romans 6:23)

For this is how much God loved you, _____ (your name): He gave His only Son, Jesus, so that if you believe in Him, you will not perish but have eternal life. (John 3:16)

Jesus gave His life for your sins, _____ (your name), to rescue you from this evil world in which we live. (Galatians 1:4)

~

_____ (your name), Jesus is your Rescuer.

Chapter 7:
Ambush Under the Sea

"Elizabeth, why did you go out in the storm?" asked Jacob.

"I just wanted to see if the sea turtle eggs were okay," she answered. "But the waves were too high."

"And you *won't* do that again, right?" said Stephen.

"Right," Elizabeth groaned. "That was awful!"

"Elizabeth, honey, you scared us half to death," said Martha. "Thank the Lord you're okay. Now, don't worry about those eggs. It's supposed to clear up tomorrow. Hopefully we can get back on the beach then to check the nest. But in the meantime, trust God. He's worthy, you know."

"Papaw, what are we gonna do today since it's raining?" asked Isaac.

"Anybody wanna go shoppin' for souvenirs?" asked Wilbur.

"Yes!" the children cheered.

~

POUND!

POUND!

POUND!

Ocean waves hammered the boardwalk. Izzy popped from under the dripping planks and zipped over the sand dunes to a sea-oat shelter near the beach house.

Cindy's copious amounts of cold, fresh-water rain poured into the perilous waves, reducing the temperature and salinity of the near-surface water. Larger marine sharks and dolphins swam deeper and farther out into the gulf to escape the rough-and-tumble currents clobbering smaller fish, crabs, and Marina's nest. Inch by inch, the mound of sand protecting the clutch swept away. The odds against the pre-hatchlings' survival appeared overwhelming.

According to wildlife studies, only a small remnant of sea turtle eggs – sometimes as few as ten out of one hundred – survive predators and life-threatening elements, and of the survivors, one out of 1,000 baby sea turtles commonly live to adulthood. If Marina's eggs washed out to sea, their chance of survival would plummet to zero.

Seven hundred miles away off the coast of Sanibel Island in southwest Florida, Marina faced her own survival threat: a bloodthirsty bull shark (fittingly named for its stocky shape and aggressive nature). Since bull sharks hunt in tropical shorelines where people often swim, experts consider them the most dangerous sharks in the world. Most live in saltwater, but because these powerful predators have developed the ability to keep salt in their bodies, they've also invaded fresh-water estuaries, rivers, and lakes.

The eight-foot predator moved silently over the sandy seafloor. Although its primary diet consists of bony fish and smaller sharks, today, the fearless, opportunistic hunter targeted the large loggerhead grazing in the seagrass a few yards ahead.

Unaware of the approaching danger, Marina leisurely cropped tender blades like a lawn mower. Sea-turtle pruning not only fills hungry bellies, but also stimulates the grass roots to grow a healthier underwater pasture.

The gray shark circled its prey – the first action before the characteristic "bump and bite" attack. Like her pre-hatchlings under the battered Fort Morgan Beach, the odds against Marina's survival appeared overwhelming. Her sole natural defense is her hard shell, and her lone chance for survival is strategic maneuvers to outsmart the enemy.

BUMP!

Before the shark's deathly bite, the turtle quickly rolled sideways, using her carapace as a shield and presenting her full width before the open jaws. Had she remained horizontal, one powerful bite of those sharp teeth would have ended her life. The shark's mouth could not open wide enough to bite the vertical turtle, so he circled again.

BUMP!

When hit a second time, Marina once more flipped on her side and offered her wide, hard shell before the predator's deadly jaws. The shark circled for the third attack.

This time, the sea turtle took advantage of her shorter length, swam out of harm's way under the attacker's white belly, and turned tighter circles than the twirling assailant. Unable to reach Marina, the bull shark refocused on a passing stingray and sped north toward Captiva Island and his latest victim.

Marina pumped her front flippers and swam southeast toward the Sanibel Lighthouse – a ninety-eight-foot, kerosene-powered lighthouse at Point Ybel on the end of the twelve-mile barrier island. It was built in 1884 to mark the entrance of San Carlos Bay as well as attract travelers and more trade.

The turtle climbed to the surface and breathed. Marina had won today's battle for life, but at Fort Morgan, the crushing waves ripped the last layer of sand from her endangered clutch.

REFLECTIONS

_____ (your name), to win life's battles, you must put on God's armor and exercise His winning strategies.

~

_____ (your name), be strong in the Me and in My mighty power. Put on all of My ARMOR so that you will be able to stand firm against all strategies of the devil. For you are not fighting against flesh-and-blood enemies, but against evil and mighty powers in this dark world. (Ephesians 6:10-12)

_____ (your name), stand your ground, putting on the belt of TRUTH and the body armor of My RIGHTEOUSNESS. For shoes, put on the PEACE that comes from the Good News so that you will be fully prepared. (Ephesians 6:14-15)

_____ (your name), hold up the shield of FAITH to stop the fiery arrows of the devil. Put on SALVATION as your helmet, and take the sword of the Spirit, which is My WORD. Stay alert and be persistent in PRAYER. (Ephesians 6:16-18)

~

_____ (your name), stand strong in God's armor.

Chapter 8:
Catastrophe

"Okay, everybody gets one souvenir," instructed Wilbur. "Parents, stay with your kids, and everybody meet me at the register in thirty minutes."

"What's for supper?" asked Dan.

"Seafood, dear," said Martha.

"Yes, ma'am, but *where* are we goin' for supper?" asked Dan.

"Let's see. Tonight's Ben and Gabriela's turn to pick," said Martha.

"We're still tryin' to decide," said Ben.

"Let's go early, so we'll beat the crowds," said Dan.

"We'll tell you our pick when we meet at the register," promised Gabriela.

"Time's a-wastin'," said Wilbur. "Better get to shoppin'."

~

A savage wave unlocked Marina's flask-shaped chamber, exposing the ping-pong-ball-sized eggs at the top of the clutch, and dragged five, precious eggs out to sea.

~

"What are you gonna get, Mamaw?" asked Elizabeth.

"A T-shirt," said Martha.

"That's what you got the last time we came to the beach," said Elizabeth.

Martha laughed. "That's what I get *every* time we come to the beach. What are you getting?"

"I want a T-shirt, too," said Elizabeth, "the airbrush kind."

"Those are pretty. Let's go see the designs they have to choose from," said Martha. "Elizabeth, you're always the first one to choose a souvenir."

Elizabeth grinned.

~

A weaker surge stopped inches short of the one-hundred-and-four-egg clutch.

~

"Dad, you wanna go look at the hats?" said Jacob.

"Sure," said Stephen.

Isaac dug through a wire bin of super balls, and little Alexander and baby Hunter pulled toy cars from a bottom shelf. Baby Lee found a large dump truck filled with beach toys.

"Bi tuck!" he said.

"Yeah, that is a big truck," said Dan.

~

CRASH!

Water engulfed the sea turtle nest, and fifteen eggs floated away in the retreating deluge.

~

"Everybody put your treasures on the counter," said Wilbur.

"Is this all on one ticket, sir?" asked the cashier.

"Yep," said Wilbur.

"Young lady, when you have children, just remember, they multiply," said Martha sweetly.

"Yes, ma'am," said the wide-eyed teenager.

~

Eighty-nine eggs bobbed in the flooded hole.

~

"It's 4:30. Where are we goin' for supper?" asked Dan.

"Ocean View. It has great food, and the kids will love the gigantic, saltwater aquarium," said Gabriela. "It's really cool."

"Everybody know how to get there?" asked Wilbur.

The guys held up their phones.

"GPS," said Ben.

"Okie dokie. Let's go then," said Martha.

~

Another wave snatched forty-three eggs and violently flung them into the churning sea.

~

Isaac held little Alexander's hand and pointed to a bright orange and white fish weaving in and out of a coral castle in the oversized aquarium.

"Clownfish!" said Alexander.

"How'd you know that?" asked Isaac.

"I love the purple tangs with the yellow tails," said Rebekah.

"The lionfish are really cool," said Stephen.

"Rrr," growled baby Lee.

"Grrr," baby Hunter parroted.

"I like the starfish," said Elizabeth.

"Oh, wow!" said Amanda. "Look at that one. It's so colorful. What's it called?"

"I think it's called a dragonet," said Ben.

"Food's here," called Martha. "Time to eat. Did everyone wash your hands after the souvenir store?"

~

In the moonless night, Tropical Depression Cindy pushed northward into the Ohio and Tennessee valleys. Whirling winds calmed. The downpour ebbed to a drizzle. Izzy shivered in the darkness beside Marina's nest –

BEATEN.

BATTERED.

TORN.

EMPTY.

REFLECTIONS

When calamity strikes, _____ (your name),

God is with you.

~

_____ (your name), I am your refuge

and strength, always ready to help in times of trouble. (Psalm 46:1)

_____ (your name), your help comes

from Me who made heaven and earth! (Psalm 121:2)

So, _____ (your name), do not fear when

earthquakes come and mountains crumble into the sea. I, the

LORD of Heaven's Armies, am there among you; I am your

fortress. (Psalm 46:2,7)

~

When calamity strikes, _____ (your

name), stay close to God.

Chapter 9:
Why?

Day Fifty-two.

"Hello, Holly?" said Martha the following morning. "This is Martha Willowkins from Waves and Waffles beach house in Fort Morgan. I'm so sorry to tell you that the storm ripped your canopies to shreds. What should we do?"

"Hi, Martha," said Holly. "Yes, ma'am, my bad. We took down the rentals in Gulf Shores before the storm, but unfortunately didn't make it out to Fort Morgan. We'll come down later today and set up new ones for you."

"Oh, thank you, dear," said Martha. "And again, I'm so sorry for your loss. Bye, now."

Wilbur called from the balcony, "I see patches of blue peeking through the gray. It's clearing up."

"Can we go to the beach and check on the turtle nest?" begged Elizabeth.

"Let's finish breakfast first and help Mamaw clean up; then we'll go," Rebekah promised.

"I hope the eggs are okay," Elizabeth sighed.

After breakfast, mothers smeared sunscreen on the children.

"Why do we have to put on suntan lotion?" asked Isaac. "The sun's not out."

"Harmful rays still come through, buddy, even when it's cloudy," said Rebekah. "And besides, maybe the sun *will* shine before we leave the beach."

Elizabeth ran to the yellow marker leaning over a gaping hole.

"They're gone!" she wailed. "The nest is empty!"

"Oh, no! Are you sure?" asked Martha. "Let's see."

Martha knelt beside her granddaughter and carefully dug into the barren pit.

"I'm so sorry, sugar," Martha said and hugged the heartbroken little girl. "It looks like the eggs washed out to sea."

Elizabeth sniffed. "Mamaw, why did God let 'em wash away? I prayed like you told me to, and I trusted God to take care of the eggs like you said. But He didn't answer my prayers."

"Oh, honey, our heavenly Father always answers our prayers, but sometimes His answer is no. That's when we need to trust Him the most," said Martha.

"But why would He say no? The baby turtles didn't do anything wrong," she sniveled. "I don't think Jesus loves me. He would've answered my prayers if He cared."

"Elizabeth, that's not true! Jesus loves you very, very much," said Martha.

The little girl stared at her bare toes.

"I know it's hard to understand, sugar," Martha continued, "but you need to learn that God is very good and loving when He says yes to our prayers, and He's very good and loving when He says no. We live in a topsy-turvy world tarnished by sin. So, there's gonna be sickness and death and sorrows and tropical storms until God sets everything back right again. Jesus warned us that we'd face troubles. Why, even *He* suffered on this earth, and Jesus is God's Son. A wise, Old Testament prophet named Habakkuk wrote, *'Even though the olive crop fails, and the fields lie empty and barren; even though the flocks die in the fields, and the cattle barns are empty, yet I will rejoice in the LORD! I will be joyful in the God of my salvation!'"*

SILENCE.

Martha pointed to the ocean. "See those big waves?"

Elizabeth nodded.

"They tell a story of great trust in God's love."

"How?" asked Elizabeth.

"Well, long, long ago, a man lost his little son, and very soon after that, he lost much of his wealth and fortunes in the Great

Chicago Fire of 1871. Only two years later, a ship carrying the man's wife and four daughters collided with another sea vessel and sank in minutes. Only his wife survived. While crossing the cruel Atlantic to meet his grieving wife, Horatio Spafford wrote a hymn that goes like this…"

Martha sang,

> *"When peace, like a river, attendeth my way,*
>
> *When sorrows like sea billows roll;*
>
> *Whatever my lot, Thou has taught me to say,*
>
> *It is well, it is well with my soul.*

> *And, Lord, haste the day when the faith shall be sight,*
>
> *The clouds be roll'd back as a scroll,*
>
> *The trump shall resound, and the Lord shall descend,*
>
> *"Even so," it is well with my soul."*[1]

"Never doubt God's love for you, honey. He loves you so much that He sent Jesus, His only Son, to rescue you and me and

---

[1] IT IS WELL WITH MY SOUL. Horatio G. Spafford, 1873.

people all around this old, broken world from our many sins. The Bible says, *'Jesus gave His life for our sins, just as the Father planned, in order to rescue us from this evil world in which we live.'* People and sea turtles and all of creation…"

"And Izzy?" interrupted Elizabeth.

Martha nodded. "Yes, and Izzy - we're all eagerly waiting for a future day when we'll join the Lord in glorious freedom from sin and death and pain and suffering. No matter what happens in life – good or bad – God loves you, and God is always good. He deserves your trust, Elizabeth, even when sorrows like sea billows roll."

REFLECTIONS

_____ (your name), you live in a topsy-turvy world tarnished by sin.

~

_____ (your name), whatever you suffer now is nothing compared to the glory I will reveal to you later. (Romans 8:18)

_____ (your name), when you think of your suffering and awful times, dare to have hope in Me. (Lamentations 3:19-21)

My faithful love never ends, _____ (your name). My mercies never cease. Great is My faithfulness; My mercies begin afresh each morning. Therefore, have hope in Me! (Lamentations 3:22-24)

~

When God says no to your prayers, _____ (your name), trust that He loves you, He is with you, and He's up to something good – even when sorrows like sea billows roll.

Chapter 10:
Ping-Pong Balls

"The rental people are here," called Ben. "Look, they brought their dogs."

"What are your dogs' names?" asked Jacob. "Can we pet 'em?"

"The brown one's Gumbo, and the black and white is Thibodaux," said Holly. "Sure, you can pet 'em. They're really friendly."

"Thibodaux?" asked Martha. "Are you from Louisiana? We lived in Bogalusa, Louisiana for ten years when our kids were little."

"No, ma'am," she said. "But my grandparents live there, and I liked the name."

Wilbur flipped an indigo-blue Frisbee to Jacob, and Gumbo took off like a racehorse out of the gate.

"Looks like you've got a good Frisbee dog," said Wilbur. "When Martha and I first married, we had an Australian shepherd named Butch that was a great Frisbee dog."

"Gumbo chases anything you'll throw," said Mike, Holly's assistant.

Gumbo chased the Frisbee. Thibodaux chased Gumbo. The children chased Thibodaux. Izzy watched the race from the boardwalk and then darted toward the ravaged nest. She slipped past Martha's toes, circled the sandy crater, and searched...

WEST.

EAST.

NORTH.

Izzy hesitated a moment and then dashed...

SOUTH.

The tiny lizard stopped beside a round, white ball.

"Look, Mama," cried Rebekah, "there's Izzy! Come see, Elizabeth. Izzy's back."

"Izzy!" Elizabeth squealed.

The little girl ran to Martha. Her blue eyes sparkled with joy.

"Mamaw, I asked God to protect Izzy, and He said yes! Mom, found her."

"Thank You, Jesus!" Martha shouted.

"That's weird," Rebekah said. "Izzy's sitting by a ping pong ball."

"Here's another one," said Jacob.

"Those aren't ping pong balls, silly," said Stephen. "Those are eggs."

"Sea turtle eggs?" cried Elizabeth. "Oh, my goodness. It's sea turtle eggs!"

"Everybody come quick!" shouted Jacob. "We found turtle eggs."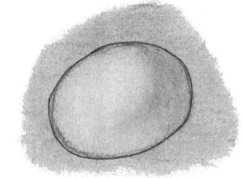

"Grab the dogs!" yelled Stephen. "Don't let 'em get the eggs."

Dan whistled. "Here Gumbo. Here Thibodaux!"

He grabbed their collars and led them back to Holly and Mike.

"Call that number, Stephen," said Rebekah excitedly, "the sea turtle emergency number."

"Wait. Here comes a Baldwin County vehicle," said Stephen. "Let's ask them what to do."

Stephen flagged down two men in a black jeep patrolling the Fort Morgan beaches.

"Hi," he said. "We found some sea turtle eggs that washed out of a nest. Should we call the sea turtle emergency number?"

"That's great! We'll call for you. The turtle lady on duty should come right away," said the deputy. "In the meantime, see how many you can find. Move 'em out of reach of the tide and cover 'em with sand until she gets here. Try not to touch the eggs with your hands."

"Okay. Thanks," said Stephen.

"Thank *you* for helping an endangered species," he said.

"Anybody found more?" asked Rebekah.

"Here's a sand pail," said Martha.

Stephen carefully scooped sand and eggs with a plastic shovel and gently placed them in the bucket.

"How many have you found?" asked Ben.

"Only two," said Jacob.

"I'm so thankful!" cried Martha. "From the looks of that nest, I didn't think any survived."

"Spread out, everybody, and search the whole area," Wilbur instructed.

The beach teemed with Willowkins, Fickles, and Granny like ants over an anthill.

"I see one!" shouted Amanda.

"Where?" asked Gabriela.

"Down there – in the edge of the water. Hurry!!! The tide's pulling it out!" she cried.

"Here, buddy. Let me see your net," said Ben.

Ben snatched little Alexander's crab net and sprinted to the sea. Alexander trotted along behind him.

"Get it, Daddy!"

"Got it!" Ben hollered. "Bring the bucket."

Alexander jumped in circles. Stephen held out the orange pail, and Ben eased in the third egg.

"You think they'll still hatch?" asked Ben.

"I don't know," said Stephen. "Let's bury 'em till the turtle lady gets here."

REFLECTIONS

_____ (your name), the Lord is a wondrous God who often does the unexpected.

~

_____ (your name), I am the LORD God, who performs many wonders. My plans for you are too numerous to list. I have no equal. If you tried to recite all My wonderful deeds, you would never come to the end of them. (Psalm 40:5)

_____ (your name), no eye has seen, no ear has heard, and no mind has imagined what I have prepared for those who love Him. (1 Corinthians 2:9)

_____ (your name), I am able, through My mighty power, to work within you, to accomplish infinitely more than you might ask or think. (Ephesians 3:20)

~

_____ (your name), look to God in wondrous expectancy.

Chapter 11:
The Turtle Lady

"Got it, Jim," said Jenn. "I'll be there in about twenty minutes. Tell them to cover the eggs with sand till I get there."

"I did," said Jim.

"Great. Thanks. Bye now."

Jenn opened the hatch of the silver SUV. "Bucket, wire, stakes, flagging, gloves, measuring tape, rubber mallet," she muttered. "That should do it."

For five years, Jennifer Morrison had worked with "Share the Beach" – a volunteer organization that educates the public, patrols the beaches, marks sea turtle nests, and even serves as nighttime nest-sitters to ensure the hatchlings' safe journey to the sea.

Jenn parked beside the boardwalk. The children ran to greet her.

"Are you the turtle lady?" asked Isaac.

"Yes, I am - one of many," said Jenn. "My name's Jenn. What's yours?"

"Isaac," he answered.

"So, Isaac, I heard you found some sea turtle eggs."

"Just three," said Elizabeth.

"We thought they were ping pong balls," said Jacob. "The storm washed the nest away."

"Well, let's rebuild the nest for the triplets," said Jenn.

Stephen picked up the sand shovel. "We buried the eggs over here near the original nesting sight," he said. "I can dig 'em up for you, if you like."

"Thanks, but I'll use my hands," she said.

The turtle lady slipped on rubber gloves and dropped down on her knees. Izzy watched from a driftwood hideout.

"We use gloves to protect the eggs from bacteria," she told the children, "and we dig with the blunt sides of our hands instead of our fingers, so we won't puncture or damage the eggs."

She gently pushed sand away until the round tops of the eggs appeared.

"I'm glad you buried 'em close to the original site," she said. "Now that the storm surge is down, this spot should be a safe place to rebuild."

"Most nests are about eighteen inches deep," she explained. "So, let's lay these babies to one side and dig down a few more inches."

Jenn used the measuring tape to gauge the depth of the new nest. At eighteen inches, she tenderly set the eggs at the bottom of the hole and sprinkled loose sand over them until the surface lay flush with the beach. Next, the turtle lady set a wire grate over the top and tied green flagging in the center.

"What's the ribbon for?" asked Elizabeth.

"The wire keeps predators like dogs or raccoons from digging up the eggs," she explained, "and the flagging marks the center of the nest where the hatchlings will emerge. They're small enough to easily crawl through the grate."

"I saw a raccoon sniffing around the nest the night before the storm," said Jacob. "But I ran him off with my flashlight."

"Did you know that bright lights can disturb mother sea turtles and disorient hatchlings?" said Jenn. "When the hatchlings burst through the sand, which commonly happens at night, they race in a frenzy toward the brightest horizon. Natural light of the moon and stars guide them to the water, but bright, artificial lights can confuse them and cause the hatchlings to run the wrong way. So, in our sea turtle educational programs, we teach beach visitors and residents to use filtered flashlights during nesting season. Longwave or infrared lights are the least destructive. And we ask hotels and beach-house owners to guard against nightlight pollution by installing shielded, low area, longwave dark yellow or red lights."

"We didn't know that," said Isaac. "Sorry."

"Something else you can do to help the sea turtles is to fill in any holes you dig in the sand and take in beach chairs at night to make their journey to the sea safer. Also clean up trash. Turtles can mistake plastic for plants and eat it," said Jenn. "Now, let's drive a wooden stake at each corner of the grate and tie additional green flagging around the square. Then we'll staple a yellow sign to each stake, and we're done."

"According to our calculations," said Stephen, "the eggs could hatch this week. Do you think they survived?"

"The fact that they're near the end of the incubation period will increase their chances of survival," she said. "We'll have nighttime nest-sitters out here for the next couple of weeks. You're welcome to join us if you'd like."

"Can we, Dad?" Elizabeth pleaded.

"We can't stay up *all* night, but we can watch for little awhile," he promised. "But remember, we only have three more nights until we go home."

"Awww," said Jacob. "I don't wanna go home."

"Who knows? Maybe they'll hatch before you leave," said Jenn. "Thank you so much for your efforts to save the eggs. At least three little guys now have a chance to live a long life in the sea."

"How long do sea turtles live?" asked Jacob.

"It's possible for them to live eighty to one hundred years," said Jenn.

"Wow!" cried the children.

"That's even older than Papaw and Mamaw," added Elizabeth.

REFLECTIONS

_____ (your name), God can make a way where there seems to be no way.

~

_____ (your name), with God everything is possible. (Matthew 19:26)

_____ (your name), I am the LORD, who opened a way through the waters, making a dry path through the sea. (Isaiah 43:16)

_____ (your name), I am the God of great wonders! I demonstrate My power among the nations. (Psalm 77:14)

~

_____ (your name), put your hope in God – the Way-Maker.

Chapter 12:
Sea Bound

Nighttime fell over Marina's remade nest. A waxing moon glowed behind cobwebbed clouds like a lantern through thick fog.

PIP.

PIP.

PIP.

In magical unison, Rudder, Boom, and Keel pecked through the shell walls with temporary egg-tooth chisels and wiggled free into the dark, under-beach world hidden from two, vigilant nest-sitters. Two brothers and their sister unfolded and stretched from days and days in cramped quarters. The eighteen-inch dig to the surface will take the little hatchlings hours - possibly days to accomplish.

~

Day fifty-three.

A blistering sun sat in the cleared sky. Hour after hour, Rudder, Boom, and Keel frantically tunneled and rested, tunneled and rested, tunneled and rested. Tunneling with tiny flippers shifted overhead sand to underneath sand, creating an elevator-like floor that lifted them closer and closer to the surface.

TUNNEL.

REST.

TUNNEL.

REST.

~

Day fifty-four.

TUNNEL.

REST.

TUNNEL.

REST.

TUNNEL.

REST.

STOP.

WAIT.

The ruby sun slipped under the western horizon. Like Marina's innate ability to find her birth beach, Rudder, Boom, and

Keel have the innate perception to pause before entering the six-inch, hot-soil strata. The hatchlings waited for the sand to cool in the sunset.

"Can we go back to the beach?" asked Elizabeth.

"Sure," said Rebekah. "I wanna go, too."

"Let's all go," said Martha. "Remember, turn your flashlights on red since it's dark."

The family found Jenn patiently guarding the nest.

"Hey, guys," she called.

"Hi, Jenn," said Rebekah. "Any new developments?"

"Not yet," she said.

QUOK!

QUOK!

"What was that?" asked Isaac.

Jenn pointed to a bird with black head plumage, yellow legs, and grayish-blue wings fishing in the water's edge.

"That's Charlie, a black-crowned night heron," she said. "I'm keepin' an eye on him. Night herons are a threat to baby Ts.

"I won't let Charlie come near the baby turtles," Isaac resolved.

Jenn laughed. "Thanks, Isaac."

"Look!" squealed Elizabeth. "The sand's moving!!!"

Like popcorn...

RUDDER,

BOOM, and

KEEL burst from the sand.

"I think I'm gonna cry," said Amanda.

Rudder blinked sand crystals from his tiny, round eyes and scrambled through the wire grate. Keel crawled over Boom and followed Rudder. Boom, however, appeared disoriented and scuttled toward the sand dunes.

"Here you go, little fellow." Jenn picked up the hatchling with a gloved hand and set him behind the other two. "This way. Now, on your mark, get set..."

"Go!" cried little Alexander.

"And they're off," said Wilbur, watching the frenzied race to the sea.

"They're so little," said Martha.

"They're so cute!" said Gabriela. "See the baby turtles, boys?"

Hunter pointed to the little turtles. "Baby," he piped.

"I wish you could see a hundred-count race," said Jenn. "It's amazing!"

"This is pretty cool!" said Ben, videoing the racing trio.

Isaac ran ahead of the hatchlings and yelled, "Get out of here, Charlie!"

The night heron spread his wings and sailed away.

Rudder maintained the lead as the triplets scurried toward the sea as fast as their tiny flippers would move. Suddenly, a giant ghost crab exploded from the sand and snagged Keel with a front claw. The baby struggled frantically for freedom.

"Not on my watch," cried Dan, dumping a bucket of saltwater on the predator.

The crab let go. Dan picked up the marauder and dropped it in the empty bucket.

"Fast thinking, man," said Ben.

Keel hurried after her brothers.

"I didn't think about crabs threatening the babies," said Martha.

"Yeah," said Jen. "Sand crabs, fire ants, seabirds, raccoons, opossums, skunks, armadillos, even rats can attack the hatchlings as they journey to the sea. That's why we escort them to the water's edge."

"Go, little guys!" cheered Elizabeth. "You're almost there."

REFLECTIONS

Like nest-sitters for hatchlings, God is watching over you,

_____ (your name), even when you

feel like He's not.

~

_____ (your name), I, the LORD,

watch over you. I stand beside you as your protective shade.

(Psalm 121:5)

_____ (your name), the One who

watches over you will not slumber or sleep. (Psalm 121:3)

_____ (your name), I keep watch over

you as you come and go, both now and forever. (Psalm 121:8)

~

_____ (your name), God loves you and

watches over you day and night.

Chapter 13:

Out to Sea

One by one, Marina's hatchlings stepped into the salty sea to the applause and cheers of their tall and small bodyguards.

"What happens next?" asked Stephen.

"Well," said Jenn, "they'll swim constantly for several days. Scientists have tracked loggerhead hatchlings traveling as far as twenty-four miles in eight hours."

"How do they track 'em?" asked Jacob.

"With satellite transmitters," Jenn explained. "Hatchlings may swim fifty miles or more with only brief periods of rest until they find surface-floating marine algae, which provides their food and shelter for one to two years."

"So, the baby sea turtles are safe now?" said Elizabeth.

"Safe from the baking sun and land hunters, yes. But, sadly, the ocean holds its own sea-turtle predators like larger fish, tiger sharks, and killer whales," said Jenn.

"Mamaw, let's pray for the hatchlings," said Elizabeth, "and ask God to watch over them."

"That's an excellent idea, Elizabeth. Come on everybody."

In a hand-in-hand circle, Wilbur prayed, "O Lord, our Lord, how majestic is Your name. When I look at the night sky, I see the glorious work of Your fingers. For You made the heavens and the earth; You made the sea and all that is in it. Great are You, Lord, and worthy to be praised! Thank You for my beautiful family and for our new friend, Jenn. Thank You for keeping us safe through the storm and for rescuing three, little sea turtles."

"And Izzy," added Elizabeth.

Wilbur smiled. "And Izzy. We thank You for the remarkable experience of watching the hatchlings race to the sea. Please watch over them and guide them to an algae refuge. Help them grow strong and live long and one day return to Fort Morgan

Beach to birth the next generation of sea turtles. In Jesus' name we pray, Amen."

"And, Lord, no matter what happens, we will trust You," Elizabeth promised, "even if sorrows like sea billows roll."

"Amen!" everyone cheered.

Martha hugged Jenn. "Thank you so much, Jenn. Tonight was amazing! This vacation is one we'll never forget."

"Okay, kids. Show's over. Time to run get your showers," said Rebekah.

~

Beneath a star-spangled sky, Izzy slept peacefully under the boardwalk. Martha sat on the balcony listening to the lapping waves.

WHOOSH!

WHOOSH!

WHOOSH!

She scribbled in her journal:

Cordage of the cares of life twine
'Round about this heart of mine,
Creep into my thoughts at night,
Invade my soul and choke it tight.

Then one day my toes touched sand
Along the shore beside my man
And rode a bike built just for two
Then watched the sun drop out of view.

In one short while I was astounded
My vines of woe could not be founded.
Somehow, they slipped away from me
And silently drifted out to sea.

Ahhh…
How grand 'twould be to go about
With no fears, no woes, no doubt,
With mind at peace and heart at rest -
My disposition at its best.

Then these words I did recall -
An invitation for one, for all.
"Give Me your cares," my Jesus said,
"Lie down in peace upon your bed."

"For I am greater than the sea.
Let go.
Let woes
Drift up to Me."

In the dark Atlantic, Marina pushed her oversized head above the salty foam and gulped air into strong jaws and two round nostrils in a hard, thick beak.

WHOOSH!

One powerful down stroke of long, paddle-shaped fore-flippers propelled the loggerhead three body lengths forward.

WHOOSH!

WHOOSHH!

Four-and-a-quarter miles off the coast of Fort Morgan Beach, three little hatchlings swam.

AND SWAM.

AND SWAM.

AND SWAM.

AND SWAM.

The End

AFTERWORD

While vacationing at Fort Morgan Beach, Alabama in June of 2017, Tropical Storm Cindy crashed our family beach party. After her departure, we found three sea turtle eggs. A turtle lady from Share the Beach came to the rescue and rebuilt the nest. We don't know if the eggs hatched, but we hope they did.

A special thanks to Mike Reynolds of Share the Beach for checking the *Sea Billows* manuscript for sea-turtle facts accuracy and to the Share the Beach volunteers for working tirelessly to save endangered sea turtles.

And, a very heartfelt thanks to the thirty, talented, young artists that submitted entries to the student cover-art competition. In my eyes, all of you are winners! Congratulations to first-place winner: Megan Roberts, a senior at Briarwood Christian High School in Birmingham, Alabama.

Jill

About the author:

Jill Glassco began writing Christian children's books in 2011. Her fun stories offer Biblical truth to help parents bring up kids in the way they should go and have earned top-star reviews from Readers' Favorite. She and husband, Phillip, live in Birmingham, Alabama and are blessed with fourteen children and grandchildren.

Follow Jill at: www.wonderfulfamilystorybooks.blogspot.com

About the artists:

Illustrator: Anya Figert, a fifth grader at Clear Creek Christian School, loves animals, drawing, and running barefoot through the grass. She lives in Bloomington, Indiana with her parents, Rebecca and Stephen, two brothers, Easton and Fisher, and beloved pets, Lucy, Squirt, and Shiloh. Anya is an active member of Sherwood Oaks Christian Church, where her dad serves as children's ministry director.

Cover art: Megan Roberts, a senior at Briarwood Christian High School, is a gifted traditional and digital artist. Her works have appeared in "The Artisan" school magazine and the Shelby County Fair. She lives in Birmingham, Alabama with her parents, Mike and Debbie, older brother, Matt, and pets, Misty and Peaches. Megan plans to attend Samford University after graduation and is a member of Asbury United Methodist Church.

93811751R00052

Made in the USA
Columbia, SC
20 April 2018